Rabbit
and the

Not-So-Big-Bad
Wolf

by Michaël Escoffier

illustrated by Kris Di Giacomo

Holiday House / New York

For Fleurine
—M. E.

For Andrea
—K. D. G.

Text and illustrations copyright © 2012 by Kaléidoscope
First published in France as LE LOUP TRALALA in 2012 by Editions Kaléidoscope, Paris
First published in the United States of America in 2013 by Holiday House, New York
English translation copyright © 2013 by Holiday House, Inc.
Translated from the French by Grace Maccarone.
Printed and Bound in October 2012 at Tien Wah Press, Johor Bahru, Johor, Malaysia.
The text typeface is Billy Light.
The artwork w as created with mixed media,
a blend of traditional and computerized techniques.
www.holidayhouse.com
First American Edition
1 3 5 7 9 10 8 6 4 2

Library of Congress Cataloging-in-Publication Data
Escoffier, Michaël, 1970-
[Loup Tralala. English]
Rabbit and the Not-So-Big-Bad Wolf / by Michaël Escoffier ; illustrated by Kris Di Giacomo.
p. cm.
Summary: Rabbit is afraid of the Big Bad Wolf,
but the Not-So-Big-Bad Wolf brings a delightful surprise.
ISBN 978-0-8234-2813-7 (hardcover)
[1. Wolves—Fiction. 2. Rabbits—Fiction.]
I. Di Giacomo, Kris, ill. II. Title.
PZ7.E74475Rab 2013
[E]—dc23
2012027931

Tell me, Rabbit.
Do you know the
Not-So-Big-Bad Wolf?

No, that is the Big Bad Wolf.
The Not-So-Big-Bad Wolf
has small ears.

Yes, like that.
But the Not-So-Big-Bad Wolf
has small teeth.

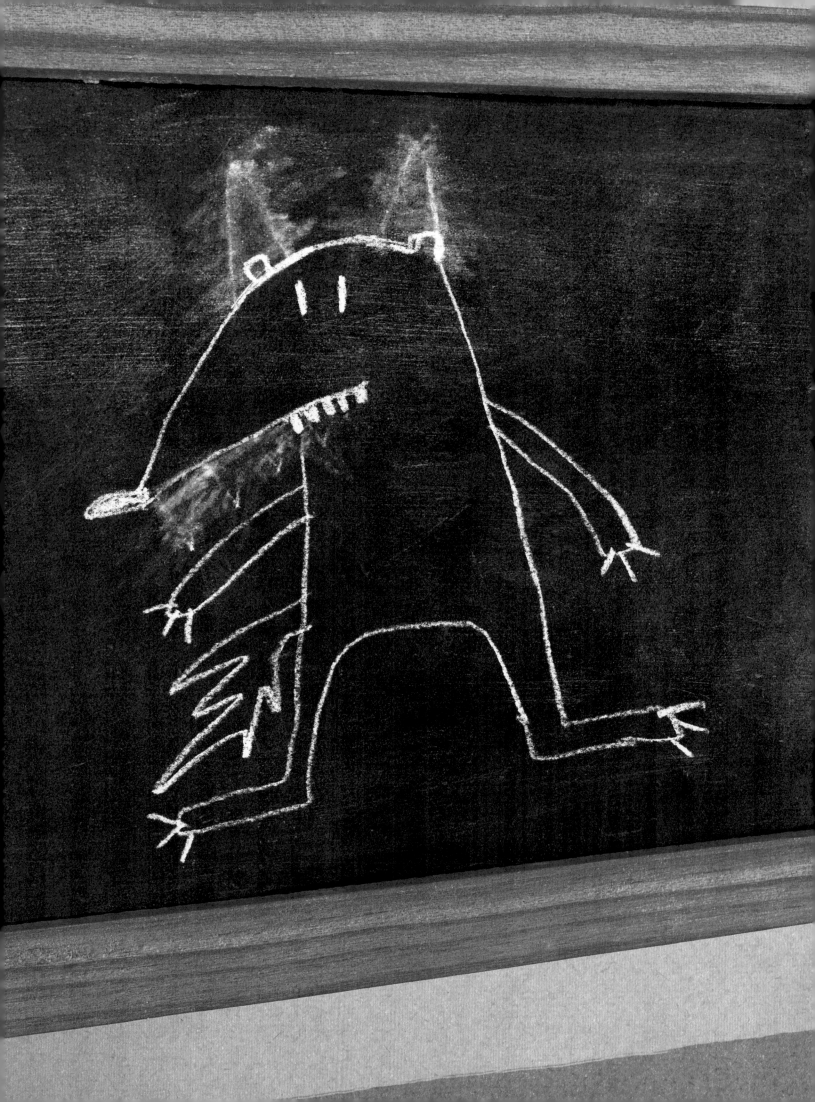

That's good.
But the Not-So-Big-Bad Wolf
has a small nose.

Almost.
But the Not-So-Big-Bad Wolf
has long hair.

Yes. The Not-So-Big-Bad Wolf
looks like that.
And here it comes!

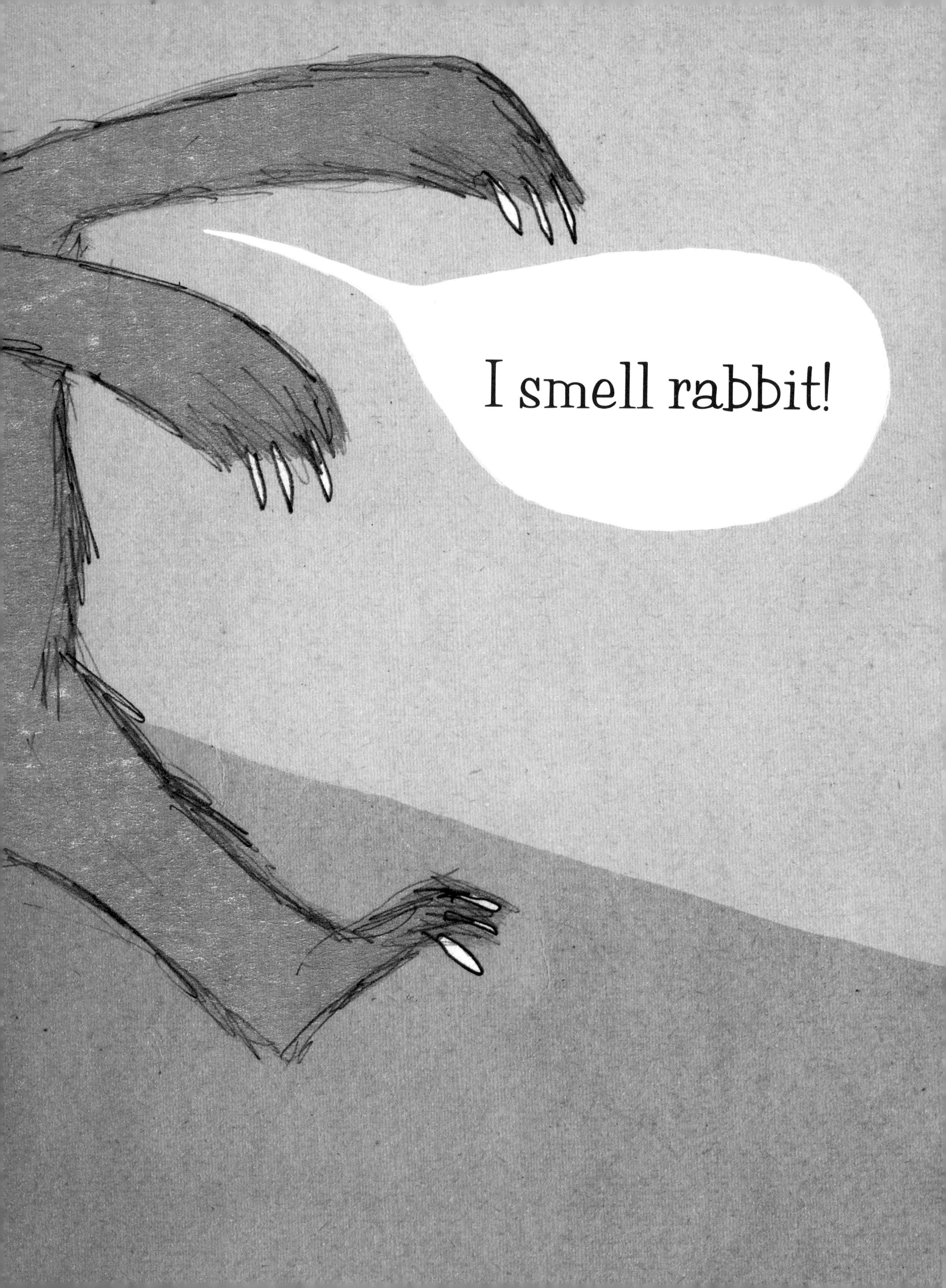
I smell rabbit!

Don't let it
catch you. Hide!

Not there.
The wolf can see your ears.

Not there.
The wolf can see your tail.

Too late!

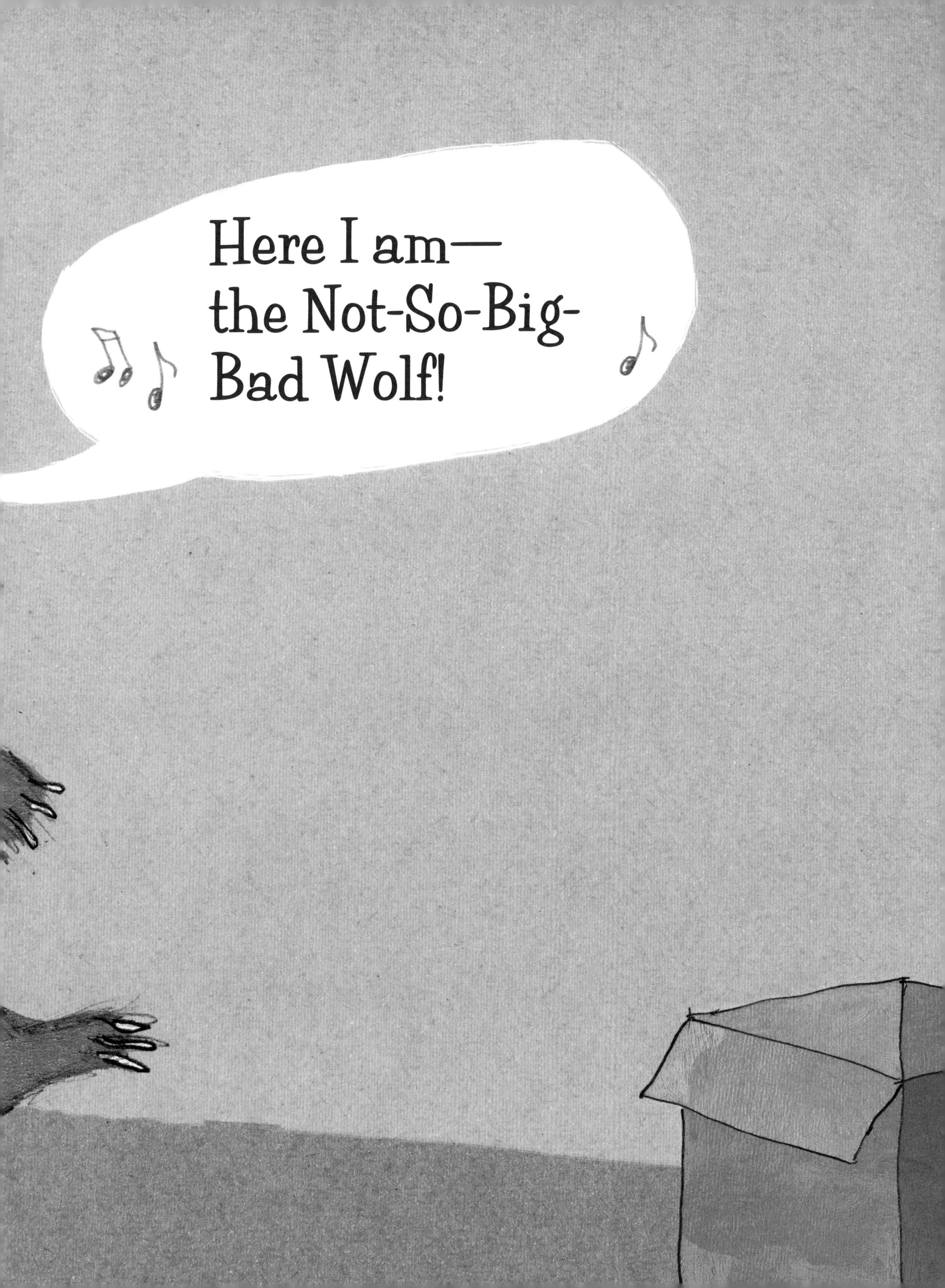
Here I am—
the Not-So-Big-
Bad Wolf!

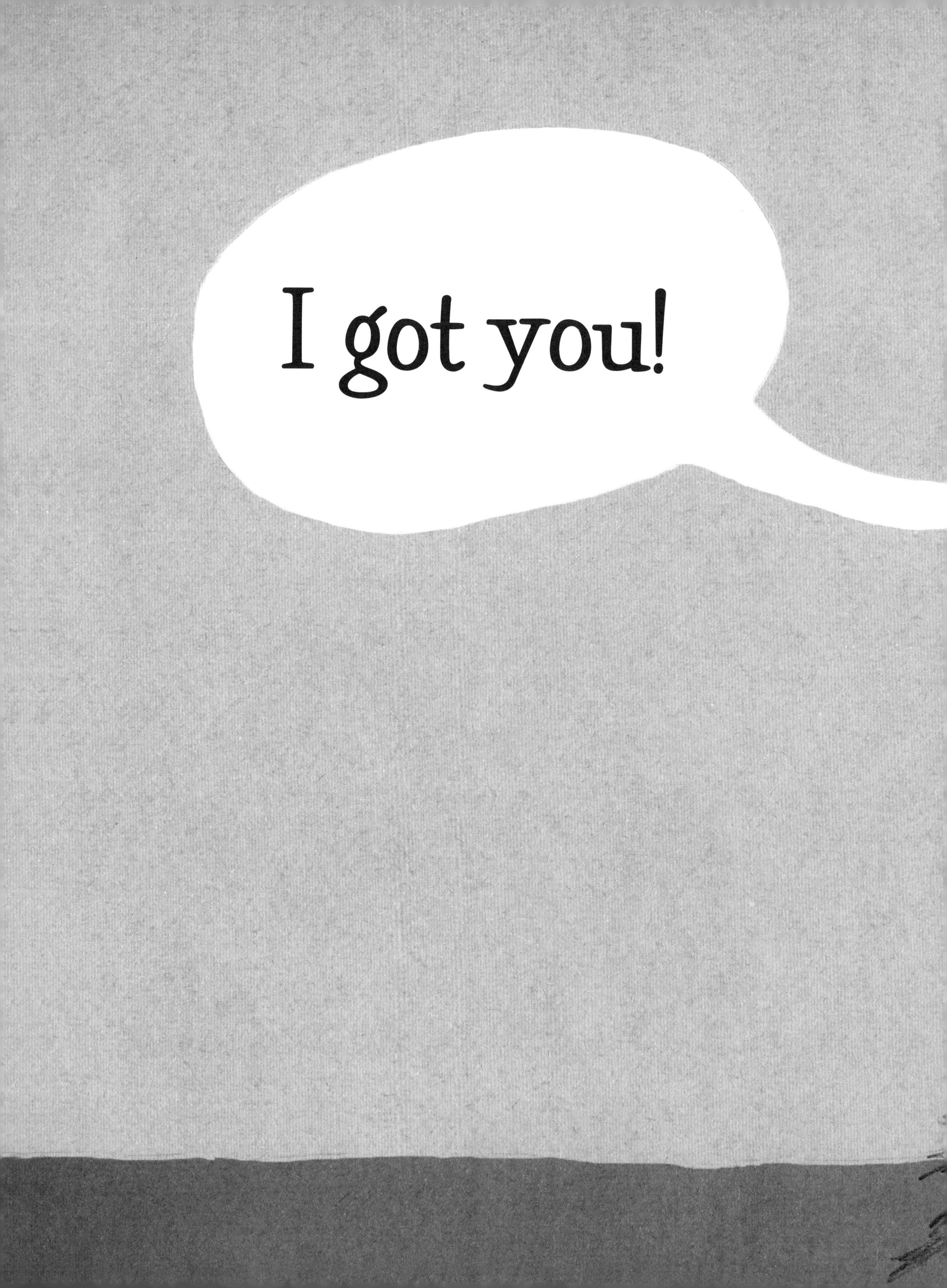
I got you!

And now
you will get
a big hug!